우리 문학은 우리 문화의 또 다른 창입니다. 한림 출판사는 한국 현대 단편 문학의 숨은 보석과 같은 작품들을 엄선, '글' 과 더불어 조화로운 이중주를 연주하기 위한 '그림' 작업을 더하여 세계의 관객을 향해 다가가고자 합니다. 우리의 '한글' 과 더불어 세계인과 소통할 수 있는 '영어' 와의 이중주를 통해 세계의 무대 위에 서서 우리의 이야기를 시작하고자 합니다. Literature often offers readers a special window into a country's culture. This is especially true in Korea's case, which is in part why Hollym is proud to be associated with this special project that provides readers with a collection of stories presented in both English and Korean, with accompanying illustrations, as it will help people from around the world better understand Korea's time-honored and unique culture. At the same time, it will expose a new generation of readers to many of Korea's most respected authors and short stories.

작가 이문열은 1948년 서울 출생으로 1968년 대입 검정고시에 합격하여 서울대학 사범대 국어과에 입학하였다. 1969년 고시공부를 시작, 1970년 대학을 중퇴한 후 고시와 문단 등단에 모두 실패하자 1973년 군에 입대하였다. 1979년 동아일보 신춘문예에 중편 『새하곡(塞下曲)』이 당선되어 문단에 등단, 1979년 『사람의 아들』로 오늘의 작가상을 수상한 이래 동인문학상, 대한민국문학상, 호암예술상 등 수없이 많은 상을 수상했다. 1990년 『금시조』와 『그 해 겨울』이, 1991년 『새하곡』, 1992년 『우리들의 일그러진 영웅』이 프랑스에서 번역 출간되었고, 1992년 『금시조』가 일본에서 번역 출간되었다. Yi Mun-yol was born in Seoul, Korea in 1948. He entered the College of Education at Seoul National University in 1968 and majored in Korean Language Education. In 1970, he left the university and studied for the civil service examination until he joined the mandatory Korean army service in 1973. He received *Donga Ilbo*'s Sinchun Literature Award in 1979 for *Saehagok (Song on the Border)* and became a part of the Korean literary world. In that same year, he received Writers Today Award for *Saram-ui adeul (Son of Man)*. Since then, he has received numerous literary awards for his works. French translations of *Geumsijo (The Bird with Golden Wings), Geu hae gyeo-ul (Winter That Year), Saehagok,* and *Urideurui ilgeureojin yeong-ung (Our Twisted Hero)* were published in France in 1990, 1991, and 1992 respectively. The Japanese translation of *Geumsijo* was also published in Japan in 1992.

번역자 권경미는 Harvard University 동양학과에서 박사과정을 공부하고 있다. 2002년에는 국제교류진흥회가 지원하는 한국문학번역 펠로우쉽을 받아 오정희의 단편소설과 윤동주, 최영미 그리고 노천명의 시 번역 프로젝트에 참여했다. Kwon Kyong-Mi is a Ph. D. candidate in the Department of East Asian Languages and Civilizations at Harvard University. She received the Korean Literature Translation Fellowship in 2002 from the International Communication Foundation (ICF). Her translation projects include short stories by Oh Jung-hee and poetry by Yoon Dong-ju, Choi Young-mi, and Noh Chun-myung.

일러스트레이터 곽선영은 서울에서 태어나 미국 캘리포니아에서 자랐다. 뉴욕에 있는 School of Visual Arts를 졸업했고, 미국 West Coast Art Director's Club 금상을 수상한 바 있으며, American Illustration, 뉴욕타임즈, 보스톤 글로브, 샌프란시스코 오페라 등에 일러스트레이션 작업을 기고하였다. Kwak Sun-young grew up in California and is a graduate of School of Visual Arts in New York City. Recipient of the West Coast Art Director's Club's Gold Award, her work has appeared in *American Illustration, The New York Times, The Boston Globe,* and the San Francisco Opera.

한림 단편소설 시리즈를 기획하고 제작한 스튜디오 바프는 책의 컨셉에서부터 제작에 이르는 북프로듀싱의 전 과정을 관장하며 책의 기획에 부합하는 일관성 있는 디렉션을 통해 글과 그림과 디자인을 아우르는 일을 전문으로 하고 있다. 다수의 출판사와 기업, 미술관의 책을 기획하여 프로듀싱한 바 있다. The Hollym Short Story Series was planned and produced by studio BAF, experts in combining literary works with illustrations and designs in a manner that matches specific project goals, who oversee the entire process from conceptualization to production. They have worked on projects and produced books for numerous publishing companies, businesses, and art museums in Korea for over 10 years.

삶은 쓸쓸하다. 또는 쓸쓸하지 않다.

Life is loneliness. Or it is not loneliness.

두겹의 노래 Twofold Song

1판 1쇄 발행_ 2004년 5월 31일

지은이_ 이문열
옮긴이_ 권경미
그린이_ 곽선영
꾸민곳_ 스튜디오 바프
        프로듀서/크리에이티브 디렉터: 이나미
        진행/디자인: 김선희, 고용석

펴낸이_ 함기만
펴낸곳_ 한림출판사
        진행/편집: 이희정
등록_ 1963년 1월 18일(제1-443호)
주소_ 서울 종로구 관철동 13-13, 우편번호 110-111
전화_ (02)735-7551~4 팩스_ (02)730-5149
홈페이지_ http://www.hollym.co.kr
이메일_ info@hollym.co.kr

First published in 2004 by Hollym International Corp.
18 Donald Place, Elizabeth, NY 07208, USA
Phone: (908) 353-1655 Fax: (908) 353-1655
http://www.hollym.com

Published simultaneously in Korea by Hollym Corporation; Publishers
13-13, Gwancheol-dong, Jongno-gu, Seoul 110-111, Korea
http://www.hollym.co.kr E-mail: info@hollym.co.kr

ISBN: 1-56591-204-7
Library of Congress Control Number: 2004103834

Printed in Korea

Twofold Song

두겹의 노래

Hollym

Elizabeth, NJ · Seoul

삶은 쓸쓸하다. 또는 쓸쓸하지 않다. 쓸쓸하지 못할 것도 없다. 잔디밭에는 소녀들이 비둘기가 되어 내려앉아 있고, 허공에 뿌리박은 나무들은 잔인한 겨울의 예감으로 불안하게 일렁인다. 대지의 끝에서 불어오는 바람, 소녀들은 이제 잎새가 되어 공원의 돌담 너머로 흩어진다. 나무의 잔뿌리들이 늙은 탄금사(彈琴士)의 수염인 양 나부끼며 추억 같은 먼지를 핏기 없는 하늘에 뿌린다.

"날씨가 차군."

수의(壽衣)를 걸친 젖은 석고상같이 벤치에 기대섰던 사내가 그 곁에 허상(虛像)처럼 앉은 여인에게 축축한 목소리로 말한다. 너무 긴 사내의 오른편 다리는 세 번이나 접혀 벤치 모퉁이에 얹혀 있다. 삭아 가는 뼈 색깔의 피부에 코를 입술까지 드리운 여인은, 그러나 사내 쪽이 아니라 담 너머의 우중충한 건물을 향해 대답한다.

"마음이 춥기 때문일 거예요."

"아니야."

사내는 여인의 메마른 목소리를 흩뜨려 버리기나 하듯 단호하게 부인한다. 눈길은 어느새 여인이 보고 있는 건물에 가 있다.

Life is loneliness. Or it is not loneliness. Why should it not be loneliness? Girls become doves and sit on the lawn, and trees rooted in the air toss about with the premonition of a vicious winter. Wind blows from the ends of the earth, and the girls now become leaves and scatter on the other side of the stone wall enclosing the park. Fine roots flutter in the wind like an old *geomungo* player's beard, raising reminiscent dust to the pale sky.

"It's cold."

The man who has been leaning on the bench like a wet plaster statue covered by a shroud murmurs in a damp voice to the woman sitting down beside him like an illusion. His right leg is too long; it is folded three times and rests on the edge of the bench. The woman, her skin the color of rotting bone and her nose drooping down to her mouth, replies not toward the man but toward

"저기를 봐. 눈이 오고 있잖아?"

"하지만 그 꼭대기를 봐요, 햇빛이 눈부시지 않아요?"

여인은 약간 호소하는 말투다. 그러나 사내는 오히려 그 당돌함에 흠칫하며 한동안 말이 없다가 이내 머리를 끄덕인다.

"그렇군. 햇빛을 받아 온통 금빛이군."

"네, 정말 눈이에요. 건물 밑동은 이미 거멓게 젖어 오고 있군요."

사내가 서서히 말을 바꾸자 여인도 까닭 없이 풀이 죽으며 이번에는 자기의 말을 뒤집는다. 하지만 금빛으로 번쩍인다 해서 차가움의 반대라고는 할 수 없지, 내일 다시 떠올라야 할 피로가 우연히 건물 꼭대기에 얼룩진 것뿐이야, 라고 말해 주고 싶던 사내는 거기서 문득 할 말을 잊는다.

그사이 그들이 보고 있는 건물은 조용히 그날 몫을 가라앉힌다. 도회의 그쪽은 매일 한 자씩 땅 속으로 꺼져 든다. 들리기에 사람들이 그 밑에서 너무 많은 것을 파내 땅 위에다 쌓았기 때문이라고 한다. 그 자리, 아득한 옛날에 석회(石灰)의 강물이 흘러가고, 다시 그 위를 열 길이나 되는 고사리가 무성하던 자리. 몇천 년 전에는 늙은 소나무들이 비

the gloomy building beyond the stone wall.

"Probably because your heart is cold."

"Not at all," he denies adamantly, trying to diffuse the woman's dry voice. His eyes fixate on the same building that the woman is gazing at, "Look, look over there. It's snowing, isn't it?"

"But look at its rooftop. Isn't the sunlight radiant?" she pleads a little.

The man does not respond immediately but soon nods his head, rather taken aback by her audacity.

"You're right. It seems to glitter with golden colors in the sunlight."

"Yes, it's really snowing, and the bottom of the building has become damp and black already."

This time the woman reverses her statement with absurd dejection simply because the man has so easily changed his own. But the man who wanted to tell her, "You can't exactly say 'shining

바람에 부대끼고, 승냥이며 고라니가 떼를 지어 노닐기도 했다. 그 어디엔가 백 년 전에 지쳐 죽은 당나귀도 묻혀 있어, 만 년쯤 지나면 사람들은 그 뼈를 유리그릇에 담아 늘어놓을 것이다.

"생각나세요?"

문득 그리움을 충동질하는 눈길로 여인이 그렇게 물어오지 않았더라면 사내는 자칫 그 당나귀 얘기를 꺼낼 뻔했다. 하지만, 생각만으로는 아무도 남을 해치지 않는다. 사내도 시치미를 떼고 그녀의 물음에 대한 성의만 표시한다.

"무얼?"

"그때 말이에요. 우리가 처음 만날 무렵."

"생각나지."

"벌써 삼 년이나 됐어요. 그날 집집마다 창틀에 활짝 핀 제라늄 분(盆)들을 내놓고 있었지요."

그렇게 말하는 여인은 이미 허상이 아니었다. 똬리 틀듯 움츠러져 있던 목은 어느새 우아하게 길어지고 입술까지 흘러내렸던 코는 꼭 한 치 위로 올라붙는다. 바람만 불면 바스러져 날아가 버릴 것 같던 머리칼에도 윤기가 비치고 삭아가는 뼈 같은 빛을 띠고 있던 뺨에는 제법 혈색까지 아른거

in gold' is the opposite of coldness. It's merely tomorrow's exhaustion smeared on top of the building," is suddenly at a loss for words.

Meanwhile, the building that the man and the woman were looking at sinks the day's share into the ground. You see, that side of the city caves in about one foot per day. They say it is because people dug up too many things from below and piled them above the earth. In ancient times a river of lime ran through this place and bracken as tall as ten feet grew thick above it. Thousands of years ago, the old pine trees wailed in rainstorms, and herds of jackals and elks roamed about. A donkey which died from fatigue a hundred years ago was also buried somewhere in that place, so in about ten thousand years people will put its bones in glass jars and display them.

"Do you remember?"

Had it not been for the suddenness of her

question and her eyes stirring longing in him, the man would have told her about the donkey. But one's thoughts cannot actually harm others, so he feigns ignorance and replies with the barest interest.

"What?"

"I mean back then, when we first met."

"Of course I remember."

"It's been three years already. On that day, each house had flower pots on its windowsills filled with geraniums in full bloom," replies the woman who is no longer an illusion. Her drooping nose shortens exactly an inch while her neck, which was crouched in a coil, becomes gracefully elongated. Her hair had initially looked as if it would fall to pieces and disintegrate in the slightest wind but now it looks lustrous. Even her cheeks, which were the color of decaying bone, gained some complexion. The man is bothered by these changes.

"I thought they were just red lanterns. Or maybe it was the dirty hem of pink curtains flapping out the window...." He reminds her in a malicious tone that this is not the time for such reflections. Yet, the woman continues more heatedly.

"You were sitting on this bench then. I sensed a lonely, scarred soul from the way you watched the gliding sunset in silence."

"It was probably the extravagant loneliness and unsatisfied desires of an ungrateful man in his midlife crisis."

"Not at all. It was loneliness and sorrow, like the scent of jasmine, which can only come from a noble and honest soul."

"It was probably the smell of twisted desire. In those days my underwear was always damp from wet dreams."

"There wasn't a single thing that could forebode

린다. 그러나 사내에게는 그 같은 변화가 마음에 거슬린다.

"나는 집집마다 붉은 등을 내건 줄 알았는데, 아니면 지저분한 분홍 커튼 자락들이 창 밖으로 휘날렸거나……."

지금은 그럴 때가 아니라는 걸 상기시키려고나 하듯 사내의 말투는 느닷없이 심술궂어진다. 그래도 여인은 열기가 더해진 목소리로 잇는다.

"당신은 이 벤치에 앉아 계셨지요. 저는 말없이 비낀 노을을 쳐다보고 있는 그 모습에서 상처받고 외로운 영혼을 느꼈어요."

"권태기에 접어든 중년 남자의 사치스러운 외로움에다 배은(背恩)과 다를 바 없는 욕구불만에 지나지 않았을 거요."

"아니에요. 고귀하고 성실한 영혼이 아니면 풍길 수 없는 재스민 향(香)과도 같은 상심과 외로움이었어요."

"그렇다면 비뚤어진 욕정의 냄새였을 테지. 그 무렵 내 속옷은 언제나 몽정(夢精)으로 축축했었지."

"이런 오늘을 예감케 하는 것은 아무 데도 없었는데……."

"어쩌면 너무 분명했기 때문에 예감조차 없었는지도 모르지."

그러다가 사내는 어느새 삭아 가는 뼈 빛깔로 돌아간 여인의 얼굴에서 늘어가는 푸른 금을 보고 불현듯 안쓰러움을 느낀다. 그 같은 대꾸는 쓸데없는 감정의 과정에 지나지 않음도. 그 바람에 사내는 앞의 말과의 연관을 거의 생각하지도 않고 성급하게 덧붙인다.

"하지만, 당신은 정말 아름다웠소. 전에 만난 적이 있다는 걸 미처 생각해 낼 수도 없었을 만큼. 그야말로 눈이 부실 지경이었지."

"시들기 직전의 처연함이 종종 꽃의 아름다움으로 착각되기도 하는 법이에요."

이번에는 여인의 앙갚음이 시작된다.

"그래도 재치 있고 발랄했어."

"늦도록 독신으로 남겨진 여자의 허세였겠지요."

"아니, 당신의 지성과 심미안은 분명 남달리 반짝이는 데가 있었소."

"남자도, 아이도 없이 삼십 년쯤 두리번거리다 보면 여자라도 이것저것 세상일을 알게 되는 수도 있죠."

그래 놓고서야 여인의 목소리가 품고 있던 칼날은 무디어진다. 입가에까지 그물처럼 덮여 있던 푸른 금들도 차츰 쓸

this day but...."

"Maybe because it was so obvious that premonitions were unnecessary."

The man merely meant to exaggerate such trivial emotions by his retort but when he notices blue cracks growing again on her now-ashen face, he becomes sympathetic. Without considering the relevance to his preceding comment, he rushes to add, "But you were really beautiful. So beautiful that I couldn't even remember we'd met before. You simply dazzled me."

"A flower's sorrow just before it withers is often mistaken for beauty."

Now the woman begins her retaliation.

"But still, you were witty and full of life."

"You mean it was the bluff of an old spinster."

"No, your intelligence definitely stood out and shined way above the others."

"Even a woman can learn a few things about life

쓸한 미소로 바뀐다. 그러나 사내는 이미 물에 젖은 석고상으로 돌아간 뒤였다. 얘기하는 동안에 무심코 쭉 펴는 바람에 오른편 다리는 반 넘게 땅 속에 파묻혀 있고, 수의 같은 외투 속의 허술한 입성들은 마침 불어온 한 줄기 바람에 해져 너덜거린다. 관자놀이 어름에는 어느새 자줏빛 버섯도 하나 돋아 있다. 그걸 본 여인이 갑자기 줄어들며 말한다.

"죄송해요. 기분을 상하게 하고 싶지는 않았는데……."

"괜찮아, 나는 기분 상하지 않았소."

"아, 이런 만남으로 이끌어 가고 싶지는 않았는데……."

그러더니 여인은 문득 앞뒤 없는 비탄에 젖어들며 묻는다.

"아무것도 달라진 건 없잖아요? 도대체 그때와 무엇이 달라졌어요?"

"세월이 낭비되었소. 지나치게."

사내가 간신히 입술만 움직여 대답한다.

"그걸 낭비로만 여겨야 해요? 의미로 채웠다고 보면 안 되나요?"

"공허한 의미야."

"원래가 공허한 삶이에요."

when she's thirty years old and still wanders around without a man or a child."

Only then does her voice lose its sharpness. The blue cracks around her mouth gradually merge to form a wan smile. But the man has already changed back into a wet plaster statue. More than half of his right leg is buried deep in the ground because he inadvertently stretched it while talking. His tattered clothes underneath the shroud-like coat flutter with a single wisp of wind. A purple mushroom sprouts in the middle of his temple. Noticing this, the woman shrinks half in size and says, "I'm sorry. I didn't mean to hurt your feelings...."

"It's alright, I'm not hurt."

"Oh, I really didn't want our day to turn out like this...."

Then, struck with sudden grief, she goes on to ask, "Has anything changed? What in the world

"그래도 우리에게 함부로 공허해질 권리는 없어."

그러자 여자는 한동안 말이 없다. 그사이 하늘은 점점 검푸르게 내려앉고, 나지막한 공원의 담은 부패하는 시체 같은 고동색으로 누워 있다. 뜻밖의 새가 한 쌍 그 담을 뚫고 날아와 그들의 머리 위를 돌다 수직으로 솟아올라 검푸른 하늘을 찢고 사라진다. 무한 속으로.

"윤리가 무엇일까요?"

새를 쫓는 사내의 몽롱한 눈길이 제자리로 돌아오기를 기다려 여인이 다시 한숨처럼 묻는다.

"우리가 도덕적이 된다는 거요?"

"자유로워지는 것이지. 우리가 우리들 자신으로 충일되는 것이지."

사내가 턱없이 으스대며 답한다. 자신 있게, 그러나 곧 우울하게 정정한다.

"묶이는 것이지. 우리를 비워 남으로 채우는 것이지."

"자유로운 우리를 채우면 안 되나요?"

"그걸로는 우리의 관(棺)밖에 채우지 못해."

"그게 우리에게 새로운 세계를 보여 줘두요? 또는 낡고 억지스런 세계를 부수는 것에 지나지 않는데두요?"

has changed since then?"

"We wasted our time ... too much of it," the man replies, barely able to move his mouth.

"Was it really wasted? Can't we say we filled it with meaning?"

"Then it's empty meaning."

"Life itself is empty."

"Still, we have no right to make it empty."

While the woman remains silent, the sky descends in dark hues and the low walls—colored brown like a rotting corpse—lie still. A couple of birds pierce through the wall, circle over their heads, and soar straight to the dark sky to tear through it. Into infinity.

"What do you think ethics is?" Waiting for the man's dazed gaze following the birds to return to her, she asks again with a sigh, "That we become moral?"

"It's to become free. For us to become self-sufficient," he replies with excessive arrogance. Then, confidently but soon gloomily, he corrects himself, "It's to be bound, to empty ourselves and fill the void with others."

"Can't we fill the freed selves?"

"With those we can fill nothing but our coffins."

"Even if they show us a whole new world? Or even if they merely mean to destroy the old and unreasonable world?"

"No matter how great they are, they would only be enough to protrude from the coffin and decorate the grave to lure new coffins underground."

Although there is no wind, the clothes dangling in tatters around his shoulders fall in bits and pieces like snowflakes. A thin collarbone is bared, and the shadow of a bloody bruise appears on the spot where a rib used to be, the one said to have been stolen by a woman once upon a time.

"대단하다고 해도 관을 비어져 나와 무덤을 꾸미는 정도 겠지. 새로운 관을 땅 속으로 끌어들이기 위한."

그러나 사내의 어깨 어름에서는 해져 너덜거리던 입성들이 바람도 없는데 조각조각 눈송이처럼 흘러내린다. 앙상한 빗장뼈가 드러나고, 아득한 옛날 여자에게 빼앗겨 버렸다는 갈비뼈 자리에는 피멍 같은 그늘이 져 있다.

"우리를 비워 남으로 채우면 어떻게 되나요?"

그렇다면 할 수 없지만요, 하는 조건문(條件文)을 한숨으로 대신한 여인의 물음이다.

"오래, 편안하게 살겠지."

"그뿐인가요?"

"근엄하고 경건하게 늙을 수 있을 거야. 함부로 쓸쓸해 할 권리도 있고, 세상을 향해 큰 목소리로 떠들어도 참아 주겠지. 하지만……."

그렇게 말하는 사내의 회색빛 이마에도 검푸른 금이 거미줄처럼 어지럽게 얽힌다. 이어 목소리는 여러 개의 동굴을 거쳐서 들려오는 상처받은 짐승의 신음인 양 낮고 처량해진다.

"하지만 또……지루하고 피곤할 거야. 삶은 삼십 초마다

I guess there's nothing else we can do about it then, thinks the woman with a sigh. "What would happen if we did empty ourselves and fill the void with others?"

"We would probably live a long and comfortable life."

"Is that all?"

"We would age with dignity and piety. We would have the right to be lonely when we want, and the world would have to put up with us even as we make loud noises. But...."

Dark blue cracks tangle like a spider's web on the man's ashen forehead as his voice becomes low and mournful, like a wounded animal's groans echoing through a cave. "But still... it would be boring and exhausting. Life would become a burden we'd want to get rid of every thirty seconds."

The man feels truly dismal now, and the

한 번씩 벗어서 팽개치고 싶은 짐짝같이 느껴지겠지."

사내는 진심으로 음울하다. 듣고 있는 여인은 당연하게 또는 느닷없이 절망적으로 슬퍼진다. 금세 부스러져 내릴 듯이 푸른 잔금으로 뒤덮인 코 아래는 검고 깊은 그늘이 패이고, 열린 창문처럼 횅한 안공(眼孔) 저쪽에는 구십억의 뇌세포가 슬픔으로 파들거리는 게 보인다.

걷잡을 수 없이 자라나는 오른쪽 다리를 땅 속 깊이 눌러 박으며, 사내는 그런 여인에게서 눈길을 돌려 의미 없이 사방을 둘러본다. 조금 전의 바람에 묻어온 듯한 빨간 소년들이 한줌 짓궂은 눈길을 그들의 벤치에 뿌려 놓고 어디론가 날려 가고, 잎새처럼 가뭇없이 사라졌던 소녀들은 다시 하얀 비둘기가 되어 공원의 잔디밭에 내려앉는다. 여러 해 전에 죽은 이들의 뼈가 얼음공으로 작은 공터를 굴러다닌다.

사내의 눈길이 다시 제자리로 돌아왔을 때 여인의 몸에서 우러난 슬픔의 빛은 무슨 요염한 휘장처럼 그녀를 둘러싸고 있다. 그 엉뚱하게 선정적인 모습에 당황한 사내는 얼른 눈길을 맞은편 담벼락으로 돌린다. 그런데 고동색으로 죽어 있던 담벼락에서 갑자기 분홍빛 여인의 두 다리가 피어오른다. 이어 검붉고 거대한 수말이 그 곁에서 힘차게 달려나오

woman listening to him becomes naturally, yet hopelessly, sad. A deep dark shadow spreads beneath her nose, which is covered with fine blue cracks as if on the verge of falling to pieces. Nine billion brain cells quiver with sorrow on the other side of her eye sockets, which are as vacant as an open window.

Pushing the right leg further into the ground as it grows out of control, the man turns his gaze away from the woman to look about him aimlessly. Red boys who accompanied the new gust of wind sprinkle a handful of mischievous glances toward the bench and flitter away to another place. And the girls who had disappeared earlier like fallen leaves become white doves again and return to the lawn. The bones of those who passed away years ago roll around the small lot like an ice ball.

The man gazes back at the woman as her body

고, 오래잖아 서로 얽힌 둘은 페가수스[天馬]가 되어 천랑성(天狼星)을 향해 솟구친다. 그들을 축복하기라도 하듯 담벼락 여기저기서 금빛 팬지꽃이 피어나 순식간에 우중충한 고동색을 묻어버린다.

보고 있는 사내의 아랫도리는 까닭 모르게 달아오른다. 백열(白熱)된 귀두(龜頭)가 너덜거리는 바지 앞자락을 태우며 비어져 나온다. 상사목은 아직 시뻘겋게 달아있을 뿐이지만, 백열은 머지 않아 그 부근 전체에 번질 듯하다. 사내는 자신의 그 같은 변화가 느닷없는 탓인지, 무안함을 감추기나 하려는 듯 벤치에서 몸을 떼며 입을 연다. 한껏 심각하지만, 그 목소리에는 이미 칙칙한 고혹(蠱惑)이 깃들어 있다.

"그래도 우리는 노예고 주인이지."

여인은 아직도 푸르스름한 슬픔의 안개에 싸여 있긴 하지만, 그 슬픔은 계산된 것인 듯하다. 마치 사내의 그 같은 변화를 기다리고 있었다는 듯이나, 그 선정적인 슬픔의 휘장을 헤치고 나온다.

"맞아요. 선택당하지만 선택할 수도 있어요."

"삶을 채우는 것도 죽음을 꾸미는 것도 우리 스스로의 일

emits an aura of sorrow that envelops her like an enchanting curtain. The man averts his gaze to the wall in front of him, embarrassed by such an outrageously seductive image. Suddenly, a great red horse leaps out from between the pair of pink legs growing out of the wall which is covered with brown, dead vines. Then they intertwine with each other to transform into Pegasus, which in turn, flies toward Sirius. Golden pansies begin to blossom here and there, as if to bless the man and the woman, and spread over the tarnished wall.

Observing the changes around him, the man's crotch begins to burn until his white-hot bulbous head scorches the front of his tattered pants and juts out of them. His shaft is still red-hot but it will also be consumed by the white heat. Perhaps these changes are too sudden, the man shoves away from the bench and says, seemingly to hide his embarrassment, "But we are both masters and slaves." Though serious, his voice drips with seduction.

The woman is still wrapped in a blue fog of sorrow, but now it seems calculated. As if she had already anticipated the changes in the man, she pushes her way through the curtains of erotic sorrow. "You're right. One is chosen but one can also choose."

"It is our responsibility to fulfill life and prepare for death," replies the man.

"Ultimately we are the final judges of this land."

The single streak of vitality that just lifted her to her feet changes to a provocative flash and fills her hollow eyes. Only then does the man begin to wonder if her curtain was actually a ruse, but he is neither offended nor displeased.

"Let's go, let's leave this place first," the woman

intones.

"Yes, it looks too deserted, doesn't it?"

"You mustn't change. And now, let us head for freedom!"

"Yes, we mustn't lose the courage to take responsibility for our own choices."

"I'm not afraid, even if we will only fill the coffins in the end."

"Perhaps we will overflow them and cover the graves with roses."

"Maybe it will become a monument for the triumphal return of those who got snared in their own trap and suffered...."

The woman stands up after whispering so encouragingly that she could be accused of exaggeration.

The man yanks out his leg which was buried deep in the ground, and happily follows her. Two lovely and lustful musk deer spring out from

이지."

"이 땅의 마지막 판관(判官)은 결국 우리 자신이죠."

그리고 여인은 몸을 일으킨다. 그녀를 일으킨 한 줄기 생기는 금세 도발적인 섬광이 되어 비워버린 것 같던 두 눈을 채운다. 그제야 사내는 그녀의 휘장이 하나의 그물이었을는지 모른다는 의심에 어렴풋이 젖어들지만, 별로 불쾌한 기색은 없다.

"가요. 우선 이곳을 떠나요."

"하긴 그래. 우리가 너무 황량한 곳에 와 있군."

"변해서는 안 돼요. 자유를 향해 가요."

"맞아. 자신의 선택을 책임질 용기만 잃지 않으면 돼."

"그게 끝내는 관을 채울 뿐일지라도 두렵지 않아요."

"관을 넘쳐흘러 우리의 무덤을 온통 장미꽃으로 뒤덮을 수도 있을 거야."

"어쩌면 개선비(凱旋碑)로 남을 수도 있을 거예요. 자기가 친 덫에 걸려 고통받는 이들에겐……."

여인은 과장의 혐의를 받을 만큼 한층 고무적으로 속살거리며 앞장을 선다. 사내도 땅 속 깊이 박혀 있던 다리를 서둘러 빼내며 흔연히 뒤를 따른다. 그 둘의 발 밑에서 귀엽고

beneath their feet, hop over their heads, and disappear into nearby shrubbery.

In silence the man and the woman leave the desolate park of early winter. A uniform and a cap hanging on the gate rail wave courteously in the wind they have stirred. Only rats crawl about between the dark and hollow skeletons of the buildings. A drunken poet sings from the crumbling church steeple, swinging like laundry hanging on a washline. Alas, where is God that we are left alone in tears? Where are we that God is left alone in tears? Where did the tears go that we are left alone to make God?

This isn't it, thinks the man and stops abruptly at the corner of a secluded alley. But he escapes the pursuit of cursed thoughts with ease, strangely prompted by the woman's rosy breast floating in the limp sunset and by the black bulls' eyes glittering in the dark shadow of the

색정적인 사향노루 한 쌍이 불쑥 솟아올라 그들의 머리를 타넘고 갑자기 짙어진 부근의 관목 숲으로 사라진다.

사내와 여인은 쓸쓸한 초겨울의 공원을 말없이 빠져 나온다. 출입구 난간에 걸려 있던 제복과 제모가 그들이 일으킨 바람에 공손하게 나부낀다. 거리는 텅 비어 있고, 시커멓게 골조만 남은 건물들 사이를 들쥐 떼만 이리저리 몰려다닌다. 무너져 내리는 교회의 첨탑에 술 취한 시인이 빨래처럼 나부끼며 노래하고 있다. 아아, 신(神)은 어디 가고 우리만 남아 신을 짓고 있나……

후미진 골목 모퉁이에 이르렀을 때 사내는 잠시 이게 아닌데, 하는 표정이 되어 걸음을 멈춘다. 그러나 후줄근한 노을 속에 떠다니는 여자의 장밋빛 젖가슴과 컴컴한 건물 그늘에서 두 눈만 번쩍이는 검은 수소 떼가 묘하게 그를 충동하고, 사내는 가볍게 개뿔 같은 사유(思惟)의 추격을 벗어난다.

"뭘 하시려는 거예요?"

몇 발 옮기지 않아 다시 걸음을 멈추고 길가의 불타다 남은 가로수 그루터기에 수의 같은 외투를 거는 사내에게 여인이, 그러나 크게 이상하게 여기는 기색 없이 묻는다. 사내

buildings.

"What are you doing?" Nonchalantly, the woman turns to the man who has stopped again to hang his shroud-like coat on a burnt tree trunk on the street.

Instead of replying, however, the man crouches on the ground and begins to scrape the neatly paved road with his fingernails. The asphalt that once looked obstinate is ripped to shreds in an instant, and the man begins to peel them off, as though removing a scab from an old wound, and the crimson earth surfaces like new, raw skin from beneath the asphalt.

"What are you trying to do?" she asks again, moving closer and squatting next to the man. The fact that she knows more than she is letting on is obvious from her changed appearance. Fine red veins have faintly but surely appeared on her pale ashen cheeks, like freshwater worms in a ditch.

는 대답 대신 쭈그리고 앉더니 매끈하게 거리를 덮고 있는 아스팔트를 손톱으로 후벼파기 시작한다.

잠깐 동안에 완강하던 아스팔트는 갈기갈기 찢어지고, 사내는 오랜 상처에서 딱지를 떼듯 찢어진 아스팔트 껍질들을 하나씩 벗겨 나간다. 신기하게도 그 밑에서는 빠알간 흙이 돋아나는 새살처럼 드러난다.

"무얼 하시느냐니깐요?"

여인이 가만히 다가와 사내 곁에 나란히 쪼그리고 앉으며 되풀이해 묻는다. 그러나 전혀 모르겠다는 뜻이 아닌 것은 그사이 달라진 모습만으로도 알 만하다. 삭아 가는 뼈 빛이던 그녀의 뺨에는 수채의 실지렁이들처럼 가늘고 붉은 핏줄들이 아련히 일고 있다.

"당신과 성합(性合)을 나누었으면 해. 모든 걸 잊고, 질펀하고 흥건하게."

사내는 여전히 쇠꼬챙이 같은 손톱으로 아스팔트를 후비며 능청스레 대답한다. 지극히 근엄한 얘기를 할 때처럼 제법 이맛살까지 찌푸리며. 여인은 그런 사내의 뻔뻔스러움을 정직한 화냥기로 받아들인다.

"좋은 생각이에요. 지금 같은 때에 우리가 할 알맞은 일이

"I want to have sex with you, extravagantly and excessively, and forget everything," he replies very casually, still scraping the asphalt with his skewer-like fingernails and frowning as if discussing a very grave matter. But the woman accepts his insolence as honest wantonness.

"That's a good idea. It's the proper thing for us to do at a time like this. But here?"

"Yes, here. I'm collecting the bones of the Earth right now. I'm going to pile them up and build a wall around us since we're not supposed to have sex in front of other people."

"Then what about the roof?"

"We don't need it. There's only God above us. And anyway, wasn't someone singing about how even He's gone somewhere else?"

Yes, you're right, thinks the woman without replying to the man, so he keeps picking at the dirt, also in silence. Round pebbles in various

죠. 그런데, 여기서?"

"그래, 여기서. 나는 지금 대지의 뼈를 모으고 있어. 그걸로 돌담을 둘러쌓을 작정이지. 원래 성합은 남들이 보는 곳에서 하지 않기로 되어 있거든."

"지붕은 어떡하실 거예요?"

"그건 필요 없어. 하늘 위에 있는 것은 신뿐이니까. 하지만, 이제 그도 어디론가 가버렸다고 아까 누가 노래하지 않았어?"

여인이 정말 그렇군요, 하는 듯 입을 다물자 사내도 말없이 흙만 후빈다. 공처럼 둥글고 여러 색깔을 한 자갈들이 흙속에서 빠져 나와 사내를 중심으로 가지런한 돌담을 이루기 시작한다. 개중에는 녹색의 원뿔도 있고, 감람색의 육모기둥과 석류알 빛을 띤 육십사면체도 섞여 있다.

그런데 잠자코 그것들로 엉성한 담을 쌓고 있던 사내가 무얼 보았는지 문득 두 눈을 번쩍이며 일손을 멈춘다. 도회 저편의 지평선 끝에 떠 있던 한 조각 쪽빛 바다에 눈을 팔고 있던 여인이 호기심에 차 사내의 손안을 살핀다. 부스러지기 시작하는 은빛의 돌 조각이다.

"뭐예요?"

colors begin to rise from the earth and form a neat wall encircling the man. Among them are green cones, olive hexagonal pillars, and multifaceted objects the color of pomegranate seeds.

The man stops in the middle of building the loose stone wall with a glitter in his eyes, as if having seen something. The woman, who had turned her attention to the sliver of deep violet sea floating on the horizon on the other side of the city, is now filled with curiosity as she inspects the man's palm. It holds a small fragment of silver stone just beginning to crumble.

"What is it?"

"It was here all this time. I've been looking for it for so long."

"Well, what is it?"

"My shoulder blade. I could never find it after I was swallowed up by that tyrannosaurus. But it was buried right here all along."

"이게 여기 있었군. 오래 찾았었는데."

"뭐길래요?"

"내 어깨뼈야. 수룡(獸龍)이 나를 삼킨 뒤 영영 찾지 못했지. 그게 여기에 묻혀 있었군."

"이제 그걸 찾아 무얼 하게요?"

"내 관을 위해 필요하지. 이게 없으면 나중에 염하는 사람들이 찾을 거야. 그들은 애초부터 내게 어깨뼈 한 조각이 모자랐다는 걸 모르거든."

"그러고 보니 당신 발아래 있는 그 푸른 돌, 어디서 많이 본 것이에요."

"흔해 빠진 쑥돌 조각이야."

"그렇찮아요. 어쩌면 제가 가지고 놀다 잃어버린 노리개일 거예요. 십만 년쯤 전에."

"그게 사실이라도 원래 당신에게 속했던 건 아니지. 찾았다고 신통할 건 없어."

사내는 방금 주운 돌 조각을 어깨 살을 비집고 집어넣으며 심드렁히 말한다.

"차라리 저쪽에 가 먼지나 씻지. 공원에서 흙먼지를 눈처럼 맞고 왔잖아?"

"But what would you do with it now?"

"I need this for my coffin. Those who'll swathe me will look for it since they won't know I was missing a shoulder blade to begin with."

"Now that I look at it, the blue stone by your feet looks very familiar."

"It's just a common piece of granite."

"No, that's not true. It looks like a trinket I used to play with and lost about a hundred thousand years ago."

"It might be that, but still, it wasn't actually yours so you shouldn't be too happy you found it," he says with indifference tinged with the slightest disapproval, while shoving the stone he has just picked up into his shoulder.

"You'd better go over there and freshen up a little. Didn't you just walk through that cloud of dust in the park?" The man gazes pointedly at the waterway by the roadside.

"저건 납과 타르가 녹아 흐르는 더러운 수채예요."

여인은 사내가 자기의 말을 잘라먹은 것을 깜박 잊은 채, 그가 눈길로 가리킨 길가의 수로(水路)가 더러운 것에만 눈살을 찌푸린다. 사내는 다시 엉성한 담쌓기를 계속하면서 남의 일 말하듯 대꾸한다.

"어쨌든 먼지는 씻어질걸."

그 말에 아무런 뜻이 없다는 것은 움직임이 없는 사내의 입술보다도 이제는 거침없이 바지를 찢고 온몸을 드러낸 그의 한 발이나 되는 남근(男根)이 잘 말해 주고 있다. 그걸 본 탓인지, 여인도 정작 해야 할 일은 따로 있다는 듯이 한 꺼풀 한 꺼풀씩 허물 같은 옷을 몸에서 떼어내기 시작한다.

여인이 옷을 다 벗었을 때쯤 사내의 돌담도 완성된다. 거멓게 그을은 골조만 남은 건물들이 끝없이 늘어선 포도 한 귀퉁이에 쌓은, 사방 한 길의 낮고 알락달락한 돌담은, 그러나 기괴하기보다는 아늑하고 선정적이다. 일을 마친 사내가 서둘러 옷을 빠져나가 이제는 알몸이 되어 누워 있는 여인을 덮고, 이내 그들의 거칠고 성급한 성합은 어우러진다.

이미 수백 수십만 년을 되풀이해 온 일이라 새삼스러울 것도 없지만 시작은 언제나 황홀하다. 누구든 떨어져 보고

"But that's a filthy ditch full of melted lead and tar." She forgets for a moment that she was rudely interrupted and frowns only at the murky water.

Meanwhile, the man resumes constructing the loose stone wall and replies indifferently, "At least the dust will come off."

That he does not mean anything by what he just said is evident not from his motionless lips but from his penis, which has grown the span of two arms and torn through his pants to jut out. The woman must have seen it too because she begins to peel off her clothes layer by layer, as if having just recalled her priorities.

The man's stone wall is complete by the time the woman finishes undressing herself. About six feet long on each side, it stands at the corner of the paved road that is lined with the remnants of endless rows of smoke-stained buildings. The wall is low yet variegated, cozy and provocative

싶은 저주의 불꽃, 또는 영원히 적셔지지 않을 목마름이다. 그 고통과도 흡사한 몸서리쳐지는 열락을 향해 둘의 괴롭고 긴 허망의 행진은 시작된다.

젖은 석고 같던 사내의 몸 여기저기서는 붉게 단 강철선 같은 힘줄들이 팽팽하게 솟아나 얽히고, 푸르게 금간 삭은 뼈의 빛깔이던 여인의 피부도 뜨겁게 살아나는 핏줄들로 분홍의 꽃잎처럼 피어오른다. 어둡게 내려앉은 하늘도 그들의 머리 위에만은 에메랄드의 천장을 드리워주고 있다. 부패와 미망, 한탄과 의혹 같은 우리 삶의 여러 어둠을 간신히 헤쳐나온 자줏빛 구관조 한 마리가 돌담 위에서 운다. 포도를 굴러다니던 매머드의 턱뼈를 쪼개고 새빨간 장미꽃 한 송이도 돋아난다.

"나는 이럴 때면 언제나 까마득히 잊고 있던 고향이 떠올라, 아주 오랜 옛 고향이……."

사내가 애써 가쁜 숨을 죽이며 여인의 귀에 속삭인다. 여인이 감았던 눈을 뜨며 가만히, 그리고 열에 아홉은 건성으로 대꾸한다.

"어디게요?"

그런 여인의 갈라진 젖무덤에는 붉고 탐욕스런 혀가 널름

rather than eccentric. Hungrily eyeing the naked woman lying on the ground, the man strips his clothes and swoops down on her. And they unite in sex, with impatient violence.

There is nothing new or special about the act which has been repeated over hundreds and thousands of years, though the beginning always seems rapturous. It is a blaze of damnation into which everyone wants to fall, or a thirst that can never be quenched. So begins their long and painful march of futility toward a frightening ecstasy similar to agony.

Veins like heated steel surge up taut, wrapping around each other on various parts of the man's body, which once resembled wet plaster. The cracked and cadaverous flesh of the woman also blossoms as burning veins quickly come to life. Even the dark sagging sky lets down an emerald ceiling solely over their heads. A maroon myna which has barely escaped life's darkness—corruption, delusion, grief, and doubt—cries atop the stone wall. And a red rose sprouts, splitting a mammoth's jawbone and sending it tumbling over the road.

"At times like this I remember my homeland, the homeland I'd almost forgotten," he whispers in her ear as he tries to suppress his panting, "my old homeland from long, long ago...."

The woman opens her eyes and responds half-heartedly, in a strained voice, "Why, where was it?"

A dark red gluttonous tongue darts in and out from the crack in her bosom, and a few yellow rose mosses glitter in the bluish grey shadow of her breast.

"Past that sea, past that deep violet of primordial beginning, there is a blue-black repose. And beyond that, there is darkness and

silence. I can remember the time when I was asleep as a premonition of life there in that darkness and silence. Once out of that place, I drifted around as a lonely single cell. After that... after that I was a coral, a sea lily, a chambered nautilus, and a trilobite. Occasionally, I became a three-meter long giant sea scorpion and seized my preys with tenacious claws and devoured...."

"It sounds so long ago." The woman interrupts him again with carelessness while struggling to suppress her gasping.

"I remember what happened after that, too. I was an ammonite, an ichthyosaurus, an elasmosaurus, and then gradually.... I swam out of that deep violet primordial beginning."

"It's still too far."

"I also remember when I put on a tail and left my homeland to go ashore for the first time. Those long, long years on the Earth I spent

거리고, 청회색 젖 그늘에는 노란 채송화도 몇 송이 반짝인다.

"바다. 저 원초(原初)의 쪽빛을 지나면 검푸른 안식이 있고, 그걸 또 지나서 가면 어둠과 침묵에 이르지. 그 어둠과 침묵 속에서 한 생명의 예감으로 잠들어 있던 때를 기억할 것 같애. 그곳을 벗어나 이번에는 한 외로운 단세포로 부유(浮遊)하던 때도. 그 다음……나는 산호였고 바다백합이었고, 앵무조개였고, 삼엽충이었지. 때로는 몸길이가 삼 미터나 되는 바다전갈이 되어 억센 집게발로 그것들을 무자비하게 잡아먹기도 했어……."

"너무 까마득하군요."

여자가 다시 성의 없이 참견한다. 역시 가쁜 숨을 애써 누르며.

"그 다음도 기억하지. 나는 암모나이트였고, 어룡(魚龍)이었고, 장경룡(長勁龍)이었고—그렇게 점차……그 쪽빛 원초(原初)에서 헤어 나왔지."

"아직도 멀어요."

"또 기억해. 내가 꼬리를 달고 그 아늑한 고향을 떠나 거친 뭍으로 처음 오르던 때를. 내 몸의 따뜻함을 지키기 위해

fighting hard to protect the warmth in my body...."

His eyes fill with genuine longing as he looks into the woman's eyes, which are dancing with small flames. In them he tries to find his way back to the lost homeland of the primordial beginning. His ardent gaze reaches her heart like sunlight penetrating water's cold surface. She trembles in premonition of the blazing fire that will soon engulf her and sympathizes with his nostalgia as a sudden wave of emotion overtakes her.

"For the life of me, all I can remember is the jungle. Yes... only reckless and carefree days filled with scented fruits and soft buds. Then with a gush of wind the yellow sand blew in. The jungle came to ruin, and the distance between the trees and forests grew wider apart, blocking our road that linked one branch to another.... Since

그렇게도 어렵게 싸워 온 땅 위에서의 기나긴 세월을……."

사내의 눈은 정말로 그리움에 차 이제 막 작은 불꽃들이 지피기 시작하는 여인의 눈 속을 바라본다. 마치 거기서 잃어버린 원초의 고향으로 돌아갈 길을 찾아 내려고나 하는 듯이. 그런 사내의 간절한 눈길은 찬물 속에 스며든 햇빛처럼 똑바로 여인의 심장에 이른다. 오래잖아 자신을 사를 격렬한 불꽃의 예감에 떨면서도 여인은 까닭 모를 뭉클함을 느끼며 사내의 향수에 동조하고 만다.

"저는 아무래도 밀림밖에 떠오르지 않네요. 향긋한 열매와 보드라운 새순, 그리고 거침없던 나날의 삶만이……. 그래요. 그러다가 갑자기 바람이 불고 황사(黃沙)가 날아들기 시작했어요. 밀림은 자꾸만 황폐해지고, 숲과 숲 사이가 또는 나무와 나무 사이가 점점 멀어져 갔어요. 그것은 가지에서 가지로 이어진 안전한 우리의 길이 막혀 버렸다는 뜻이죠. 그때부터 모든 길은 땅 위로만 나게 되고, 또한 길은 바로 우리에게 위험과 피로를 나타내는 말이 되고 만 거예요. 처음 안전한 나무에서 내려와 땅에 발을 디뎠을 때는 얼마나 두렵던지……. 날카로운 발톱이나 이빨도 없고, 빨리 달리지도 하늘을 날지도 못하는 우리들은 별수 없이 무리의

then all the roads emerged on the ground and the word 'road' became something that symbolized danger and exhaustion. I was so afraid when I came down from the tree and trod on land for the first time.... Without sharp claws or fangs, without the ability to run fast or fly, we couldn't help but rely on each other to move to a new tree or a new forest, leaving behind the forests and trees we had devoured.... Perhaps you were there, too."

"I was. I was overwhelmed with joy just knowing that I had survived when I first found a new tree or a new forest. But before long, I longed for the old thick-wooded jungle and cried looking homewards."

"Even back then I always felt the jungle whenever I was in your arms. And I could surely see those rich fruits and new sprouts even on the parched branch that we would abandon the next

힘에 의지해 새로운 숲 또는 새로운 나무로 옮아가지 않을 수 없었지요. 이미 껍질까지 벗겨 먹은 숲과 나무를 떠나……아, 그때 당신도 있었던지……."

"있었어. 처음 새 숲 또는 새 나무로 옮아갔을 때는 살아남은 기쁨만으로도 감격해 어쩔 줄 몰랐지. 그러나 오래잖아 옛날의 무성하던 그 밀림을 그리워하며 그쪽을 바라보고 울었지."

"하지만, 그때에도 당신의 품에만 안겨 있으면 언제나 옛날의 밀림을 느낄 수 있었어요. 내일이면 또 버리고 옮아가야 할 메마른 나뭇가지 위에서도 어김없이 그 풍성하던 열매와 새순을 보았지요……."

"나도 보았어. 원초의 바다와 쪽빛과 그 아래 잠든 어둠을. 나는 단세포로 그곳을 부유하기도 하고, 한 생명의 예감으로 어둠과 침묵 속에 잠들기도 했지."

거기서 사내의 목소리는 완연히 헐떡임으로 변한다. 움직임도 점점 격렬해져 어깨너머로 미친 바람이 일고, 백열(白熱)은 어느 새 가슴 어름까지 번져 있다. 그의 몸은 이미 얼마 전의 젖은 석고가 아니라 하나하나 살아서 숨쉬고 외치는 수많은 세포들의 뜨거운 집합(集合)이었다.

day. . . ."

"I saw them, too: the sea of primordial beginning, the deep violet, and the darkness sleeping beneath it. I floated there as a single cell, or slept in the darkness and silence as a premonition of life."

The man starts panting again, without inhibition. His movements become increasingly violent and raise a wild wind over his shoulders. By the time the white heat spreads to his chest, his body is no longer a wet plaster but a burning assemblage of countless cells, each and every one of them living, breathing, and screaming.

By now, the woman does not hide her panting either, spewing out groan-like gasps. A small but brilliant rainbow appears around her mouth. Soon, it will rise up in a sparkling cloud. Her sweat-drenched arms, resembling gigantic pink mucus, dig into his heated spine like the tendons

여인도 더는 가쁜 숨결을 감추려 들지 않는다. 신음과도 같은 헐떡임을 토해내는 그녀의 입 언저리에는 작고 현란한 무지개가 선다. 머지않아 그 무지개는 불꽃같은 구름으로 피어오르리라. 흥건히 솟은 땀으로 분홍의 점액질같이 보이는 여인의 팔은 참나무 등걸에 박힌 겨우살이의 혁질(革質) 줄기처럼 사내의 희게 달아오른 등줄기를 파고들고, 거대한 두족류(頭足類)의 발 같은 두 다리는 보이지 않는 흡반으로 감긴 것은 무엇이든 껍질만 남겨 버리겠다는 듯 뜨거운 구리기둥 같은 사내의 아랫도리를 죄고 있다. 그들의 발치에서는 쉬고 있던 화산이 갑작스레 연기를 뿜으며 용암을 부글거린다.

"다시……보여. 원초의 쪽빛……아래 잠든 어둠. 나는— 생명의 예감이야. 단세포야."

사내가 몽환에 젖어 다시 웅얼거리고 여인도 신음 같은 소리로 그 웅얼거림을 받는다.

"보여요, 나도. 그 무성하던 밀림……지금은……우기(雨期)예요. 활엽수에 빗방울 듣는 소리가……요란하다구요……."

"떠올랐어……나는 삼엽충이야……산호야……해면이야."

in the pelt. And her legs, like a pair of giant tentacles determined to devour its prey, tighten around the man's crotch, the burning copper pillar. A volcano resting near their feet erupts in smoke and begins to seethe with torrents of lava.

"I see it... again. The deep violet of primordial beginning.... The darkness sleeping beneath it. I'm... I'm a premonition of life. I'm a single cell," he murmurs again, immersed in his own dreams.

"I see the... dense jungle, too.... It's now... the wet season," the woman moans, "the raindrops falling on the trees with large leaves... they are causing a commotion."

"I remember now... I'm a trilobite... a coral... a poriferan."

"We're... taking shelter from the rain... in the hollow... trunk of an old oak tree. You, you feel ... oh, so... warm."

"I'm an elasmosaurus. I'm a dolphin... a tuna."

"우리는……속이 빈……고목등걸에서……비를 피하고……있어요. 다, 당신의 품은……아, 따뜻……하군요."

"나는 장경룡(長勁龍)이야. 돌고래야……다랑어야."

"저는……당신에게, 꼬, 꼬리를……들어 준……원숭이……암컷이에요."

그런 둘의 신음은 점차 괴상한 울부짖음같이 변한다.

"나는 후회해. 후회해, 내가 뭍으로 기어 나온 걸. 땅 위에서 살고 싶어한 걸."

"저도……슬퍼요. 우, 우리가……나무에서……내려오게 된 게."

"언제나 강한 적들에게 쫓겨야 하고."

"주림과……추위에……시달려야 하고……."

"어쩔 수 없이 무리를 짓고."

"어리석은……규칙들을 만들고……."

"불과 도구로 허세를 부리고."

"두 발로 서서……쓸데없는……생각에 잠겨 들고……."

"언어로 해로운 기억까지 저장하고……."

"무, 문화란……허영에……젖어들고"

"스스로 만든 사슬에 묶여야 하고, 윤리와 도덕이란 이름

"I'm... to you, a female... monkey... lifting her ... tail."

The couple's groans gradually convert to wild outcries.

"I regret... I regret that I crawled ashore. That I wanted to live on the land."

"I'm... sad, too. That... we came down... from the trees."

"Always pursued by strong enemies."

"Afflicted with hunger... and cold...."

"Obliged to bind in groups."

"Making... foolish rules...."

"Bluffing with fires and tools."

"Standing on two feet ... to sink into ... worthless thoughts...."

"And even recording them in words."

"Reveling in the... vanity of... culture...."

"Shackling ourselves with our own chains... and getting wounded in the name of ethics or

으로 상처 입고."

"사랑하면서도……헤어져야 하고……."

"아, 그래 빌어먹을. 언제나 도둑처럼 만나고, 간부(姦婦)로 붙고, 빌어먹을, 배우처럼 헤어지고."

한껏 높아졌던 그들의 울부짖음은 그쯤에서 잦아지고, 오래잖아 격렬하던 움직임도 멎는다. 둘은 한동안 태엽이 풀린 자동 인형처럼 스스로가 흘린 땀과 정액 속에 꼼짝 않고 잠겨 있다. 그들이 흘린 정액과 땀은 어느새 그 돌담 안을 넘쳐 검은 내를 이루며 포도 위로 흘러내린다. 빈 콜라 깡통이 떠내려가고, 시들은 꽃다발과 구겨진 연주회의 프로그램과 좀이 슨 책과 알이 깨진 안경과 씹은 껌이 싸인 은박지가 떠내려가고—그들의 욕정과 피로와 슬픔도 떠내려간다. 고양되었던 용기와 반역도.

"날이 저물었군요."

이윽고 몸을 일으킨 여인이 돌담 밖을 내다보며 가라앉은 음성으로 입을 연다. 발치의 화산에는 검은 연기만 솟고, 에메랄드의 하늘도 사라져 버린 뒤다. 사내는 나무토막처럼 쓰러져 대답이 없다. 여인은 그런 사내를 버려 두고 돌담 곁의 수채로 간다. 여인이 정성 들여 구석구석 엉겨붙은 사내

morals."

"And breaking up even when we . . . when we love each other."

"Damn it, always sneaking around like burglars, coupling like adulterers . . . and splitting up like actors!"

When their howls wane from the peak and their violent dance comes to an end, the man and the woman sink into their own perspiration and semen like unwound puppets. This perspiration and semen soon brim over the stone wall and form a black stream on the pavement. An empty soda can drifts away as does a wilted bouquet, a crumpled concert program, a moth-eaten book, a pair of broken glasses, and chewed gum wrapped in a piece of foil—along with their passion, exhaustion, sorrow, and their heightened courage or treachery.

"It's getting dark."

The woman sits up and speaks in a solemn voice while gazing over the stone wall. The emerald sky gone, the volcano near their feet emits hazy grey smoke. The man, still as a log, does not respond. The woman starts for the ditch near the stone wall. She washes herself thoroughly of the man's semen, which has coagulated in patches all over her body. The pink heat, which was encircling her, dissipates into her flesh without leaving any trace of warmth behind.

The woman, walking back inside the stone wall, returns to her first illusion, nose drooping down to her mouth, eyes as vacant as an open window, and flesh the color of rotting bone. To that illusion, she reattaches the pieces of her skin which she had so quickly stripped off a while ago.

"Are you planning to stay here all day?" She

의 땀과 정액을 씻어내는 동안 그녀를 덮고 있던 분홍의 열기는 피부 밑으로 가는 핏줄이 되어 스며들고, 마침내는 가는 그 핏줄마저 흔적 없이 사라진다.

다시 돌담 안으로 돌아온 여인은 처음의 삭아 가는 뼈 같은 살결과, 입술까지 흘러내린 코, 그리고 열린 들창처럼 공허한 눈을 가진 허상(虛像)으로 돌아가 있다. 여인은 그 허상에다 얼마 전에 미련 없이 떼어 던졌던 허물들을 한 조각씩 주워 붙인 뒤 아직도 꼼짝 않고 누워 있는 사내에게 메마른 목소리로 묻는다.

"이대로 여기에서 주무시고 오겠어요?"

그제야 사내는 멍한 눈길로 여인을 올려다본다. 여인이 그동안 한 일을 전혀 모르고 있었다는 듯 사내는 그녀의 변모에 어리둥절한 표정을 짓는다. 그러다가 아무래도 이해할 수 없다는 투로 여인에게 묻는다.

"우리는 자유를 향해 떠나지 않았소?"

"그래요. 그래서 여기 이렇게 와 있지 않아요?"

여인은 조그마한 양보의 기색도 없이 되묻는다.

"아니, 하나의 결론으로 선택하지 않았는가 말이오? 관을 채우고 무덤을 치장하게 되더라도."

turns her icy gaze on the man who is still lying motionless.

The man stares at her blankly. Dumbfounded by her transformation and seemingly oblivious to her earlier behaviors, he barely manages to ask, "Didn't we head for freedom?"

Dismayed that the man is still in utter confusion, the woman spits out at him, "So we did and that is why we are here, isn't?"

"No, I mean, didn't we choose this for one of our conclusions? Even if it would only end up filling coffins and decorating graves...."

"That's a foolish choice. There's no notion so great that it should be chosen at the risk of our entire lives."

The man is at a loss for words but the woman goes on, "You have a name, a position, and a family to take care of. I have my own life, too. We're not masters after all, only slaves."

"그건 어리석은 선택이에요. 우리의 삶 전체를 위협당하면서까지 택해야 할 그런 대단한 관념은 없어요."

"……."

"당신에겐 지켜야 할 이름과 지위와—또 가정이 있어요. 저도 지켜야 할 삶이 따로 있구요. 결국 우리는 주인은 아니에요. 노예일 뿐이에요."

그러자 사내는 정말로 알 수 없다는 표정이 된다.

"그 생각은 방금 한 거요? 아니면 공원에서부터요?"

"그보다 훨씬 전 당신을 만나려고 집을 나서면부터예요."

"그럼 당신이 아까 말한 자유란 기껏 지난 삼 년의 연장만을 뜻했단 말이오?"

"그건 아니에요."

여인의 부정은 단호하면서도 어딘가 미안해하는 듯한 구석이 있다. 얼굴에는 다시 푸른 금들이 덮이기 시작한다.

"이게 마지막 만남이죠. 나는 그걸 꾸며줄, 오래 기억할 만한 작별의 의식을 원했을 뿐이에요. 이제 우리 어디서 만나더라도 허심한 목례로 지나쳐 갈 용기를 가지세요."

사내는 여인의 그 같은 말이 뜻밖인 모양이다. 그러나 그게 대수로운 일은 아닌 듯 그사이 젖은 석고로 돌아간 얼굴

"Did you just come up with that? Or since we were at the park?" The man is genuinely perplexed now.

"Way before then, since I left home to see you."

"Then that freedom you were talking about... did you only mean these past three years we've been together?"

"Not exactly."

Her denial is adamant yet somehow apologetic. Blue cracks begin to cover her face again.

"I simply wanted a parting ceremony for our last rendezvous so that it'd be pleasant and memorable. But from here on, let us be courageous and simply nod at each other should we ever meet again."

The man seems surprised by the woman's request. But it is not enough to coax any expression onto his face, which has returned to wet plaster. If he was affected at all, only the

minutes of silence testify to it.

"I see. In that case I must leave, too."

At last, the man gets up but instead of washing himself, he shakes vigorously like a drenched animal and gets rid of the semen and secretion that have also begun to cling to him in dry patches. Then he crawls back into the clothes he had slipped out of and becomes the wet plaster statue covered in tattered clothes. He folds the right leg, which has lengthened again, several times before hiding it inside his trousers. A thin collarbone reappears through the threadbare undergarments. The only thing that looks different about him now is his head, transparent and filled with piles of miniature books, business cards, ink bottles, and rubber stamps.

"Now that we've reached the end, I feel empty."

The fully clothed man mutters as he grabs his shroud-like coat from the burnt tree trunk. He

에는 별다른 표정이 떠오르지 않는다. 조금이라도 충격을 받은 증거가 있다면 기껏 몇 분간의 침묵 정도일까.

"알겠소. 그렇다면 나도 돌아가야지."

마침내 사내도 몸을 일으킨다. 그러나 몸을 씻는 대신 비 맞은 짐승처럼 부르르 떨어 말라붙기 시작하는 정액과 분비물을 털어 낸 뒤 빠져나왔던 옷 속으로 기어든다. 오래잖아 사내도 처음처럼 해진 옷을 걸친 젖은 석고상으로 돌아간다. 다시 늘어난 오른쪽 다리는 몇 번이나 접힌 채 바짓가랑이 속에 감추어지고, 속옷이 삭아 날려간 가슴께에는 앙상한 빗장뼈가 드러난다. 달라진 것은 다만 언제부터인가 머리칼로 덮인 부분이 투명해져 그 속에 축소된 책더미며, 명함, 잉크병, 고무도장 따위가 뒤죽박죽으로 얽혀 있는 게 내비치는 것뿐이다.

"하지만, 이게 마지막이라니 허전하군."

옷을 다 걸친 사내가 불타다 남은 가로수 그루터기에서 수의 같은 외투를 벗겨 내리며 혼잣말처럼 중얼거린다. 그리고 새삼스런 애착으로 돌담에 의지해 굳어 있는 여인을 본다. 그 순간 금세라도 머리가 부스러져 흩어질 듯 깊고 잦게 패는 이마의 푸른 금들이나, 머릿속 가득히 비치던 잡동

looks at the hardened woman leaning against the stone wall with renewed affection. Judging by the reflection of the woman's brightened face obscuring the countless black cracks on his forehead and the junk visible through his transparent head, what he said may have been more than a simple courtesy derived from a sense of obligation or common words of farewell. A small wisp of lonely grey cloud floats above his left shoulder.

"I do, too. For the past three years I have dreamt so often about being with you forever...." The woman murmurs back and a deep blue forget-me-not blooms from the crown of her head. But even that lasts only for a fleeting moment.

Out of the same anxiety, they soon regret what they have just said. First, the man adds in a dry voice, trying to retract his own absurd sentiments, "Not because I can't hold you anymore, but

사니 대신 여인의 밝게 핀 얼굴이 자리잡는 것으로 보아 그의 말이 단순한 의무감에서 나온 의례적인 것이나 이별의 상투어 같지만은 않다. 왼쪽 어깨 위에는 작고 쓸쓸한 회색 구름 한 덩이도 떠 있다.

"저두요. 지난 삼 년 그렇게도 자주 당신과 영원히 함께가 되는 꿈을 꾸곤 했었는데……."

역시 혼잣말처럼 중얼거리는 여인의 정수리 위에는 남청색의 물망초 한 송이가 돋아난다. 그러나 그것도 잠시였다. 둘은 곧 똑같은 두려움으로 자신이 한 말을 후회한다. 사내가 먼저 자신의 터무니없는 감상을 철회하는 듯, 메말라진 목소리로 덧붙인다.

"더 이상 당신을 안을 수 없다는 것 때문이 아니라—이제 다시는 여자를 사랑할 수 없게 되리라는 예감 때문일 거야."

"마찬가지예요. 저도 당신을 다시 만나지 못한다는 사실보다 제가 혼자 남게 되었다는 게 슬퍼요."

그러자 사내의 자세는 약간 느슨해진다.

"떠나야 할 때를 알고 떠나는 사람의 뒷모습은 얼마나 아름다운가……. 당신은 좋은 여자였어."

"당신두요."

because of the premonition that I won't ever be able to love a woman again."

"I feel the same way. I'm sad not because I won't be able to see you anymore but because I'll be alone."

The man relaxes only then to exclaim, albeit too profoundly, "How beautiful is the back of a woman who leaves knowing her time has come.... You were a good woman."

"As you were a good man."

"You were a saint... a temptress."

"And you, a knight and a villain."

"A blessing... and a curse."

"A joy and an affliction."

"Intoxication and disillusionment."

"Every song is twofold."

Finally, the woman moves away from the stone wall and approaches the man. "Here, let's go now, it's getting late. But before you say goodbye, won't

"성녀(聖女)였고……요부였지."

"기사(騎士)이고 치한이었지요."

"축복이고……저주이기도 했지."

"기쁨인 동시에 괴로움이었지요."

"도취이고 환멸이었지."

"모든 노래는 두 겹이지요."

여인은 그렇게 말을 맺고는 기대섰던 돌담에서 떨어져 남자에게로 다가간다.

"자, 이제 그만 나가요. 너무 늦었어요. 그 전에 마지막 입맞춤을 해주시지 않겠어요?"

어느새 두 눈은 가동중인 컴퓨터의 신호용 램프처럼 파랗게 깜박이고, 목소리는 무거움을 털어 버린 채다. 사내가 조립한 로봇처럼 직각으로 움직이며 말없이 여인의 요구에 따른다. 젖은 석고의 고동색 입술과 삭아 가는 뼈의 색깔의 입술이 부딪치며 둔탁한 소리를 낸다. 잠깐 그곳에서 분홍으로 으스름한 불기둥이 일지만 사내의 어깨에 걸려 있던 작고 쓸쓸한 회색 구름에게 자리를 내주고 만다. 떨어지는 사내의 입술은 왼쪽 모서리가 깨어져 나갔고, 여인의 입술은 남자의 고동색이 묻어나 지저분하다.

you give me one last kiss?" Her voice has lost its heaviness and her eyes sparkle like the blue flashing light on a computer's switch button.

The man moves at right angles like an assembled robot and complies with her request without a word. The dark lips of the wet plaster and the cadaverous lips of the illusion collide with a thud. A pink hazy pillar of fire rises there for a moment but ends up capitulating to the small wisp of lonely grey cloud hanging atop the man's shoulders. When the man moves away from the woman, the left corner of his dark lips chips away and tarnishes her lips.

"Goodbye, and let us remember to be courageous and simply nod at each other should we ever meet again."

The woman leaves behind these words like a lizard's tail and slips out past the stone wall. The man walks out after her, his face buried deep

"안녕. 다시 한번, 우리 어디서 만나게 되더라도 허심한 목례로 지나쳐갈 용기를 가져요."

여인이 그 말을 도마뱀의 꼬리처럼 남기고 먼저 돌담을 빠져나간다. 이어 사내도 수의 같은 외투 깃에 얼굴을 깊숙이 묻은 채 돌담을 나선다. 거리는 썩은 당나귀들과 밤이 불러낸 망령들로 붐비고 둘은 하나씩 그 물결 속으로 휩쓸려 사라진다.

강주(江州) 김씨 알지공파(派)의 십칠대 자손으로 경상북도 안동의 어떤 수몰지구에서 올라와 아슬아슬하게 서울시민이 된, 천구백육십이년 이월 십오일에 태어나 이제 스물하나로 입대를 넉 달 남기고 있으며, 학교는 고향 임천(臨川) 국민학교와 임천 중학교를 거쳐 서울의 변두리 광문(光問)상고를 일 년 반 다닌 것이 마지막이고, 그동안 받은 상으로는 국민학교 때의 개근상 세 번과 우등상 한 번에 중학교 때 받은 개근상 한 번이 있는 반면, 벌은 통금 위반으로 구류 한 번 산 일과 교통법규 위반으로 과료 오천 원을 문 것이 전부이며, 늑막염과 장티푸스를 한 번씩 앓은 적은 있지만 대체로 건강한 몸에 일 미터 칠십이 센티의 키와 육십팔 킬로그램의 몸무게를 가졌고, 흰 살결에 왼쪽 볼의 점 세

behind the lapels of his shroud-like coat. The waves of rotting donkeys and spirits summoned by the night fill the street and swallow them one at a time.

A seventeenth-generation descendant of the Aljigong branch of the Gangju Kim clan, he came from a flooded region in Andong, North Gyeongsang Province, and recently became a Seoul resident. Born on February 15, 1962, he turned twenty this year and has four months left before entering mandatory army service. He attended Imcheon primary and middle schools in his hometown of Imcheon. He then went to Gwangmun Commercial High School, located on the outskirts of Seoul, but left only after one-and-a-half years. The awards he received include one award for academic excellence and four awards for perfect attendance in primary and middle schools. The only laws he violated were a curfew and traffic regulation which resulted in detention and a 5,000 *won* fine, respectively. When he was young, he caught pleurisy and typhoid once each but he is now generally in good health. About five feet and eight inches in height and 151 pounds in weight, he has a fair complexion and three freckles on his left cheek that complement his defined eyes and nose. He was never ignored or mistreated by his female peers while growing up. Having dated various girls from a chic hairstylist to a shopping mall cashier, he even came close to courting an empty-headed college girl last spring. Considering the few hardships in his life, he is without much waywardness and is generally good-natured enough to be respectful and friendly to his superiors and co-workers. However, he still holds a few grudges about life and injustices of the world, and does not particularly try to avoid quarrels. In addition to a paycheck at the end of every month from a three-star hotel located on the outskirts of Seoul, he has tips from hotel guests and commissions from the street girls all totaling to a monthly income of at least 300,000 *won*. From this amount, he never fails to takes home 200,000 *won* to support and impress his father, who is now too old even for physical labor, and his mother, who sells various goods at a marketplace. This bellboy of room 607 at Gangseo Hotel, also called Kim Si-uk, said the following at 6:47 p. m. on November 26, 1982:

"Perverts... all that noise in broad daylight... at a time like this!"

개가 제법 뚜렷한 눈코와 어울려 또래의 처녀아이들에게 인물 가지고 서러움을 당하는 편은 아닌, 그래서 깔끔한 미용사 아가씨와 백화점의 계산대 아가씨를 각 한 번씩 애인으로 사귀어 본 적이 있고 지난 봄에는 어떤 골빈 여대생과 연애가 되다 만 적도 있는, 고생한 데 비해 구김 없는 성격에 심성도 대강은 고와 윗사람들에게는 싹싹하고 붙임성 있고 동료들 사이에도 잘 지내는 편이며, 그러나 이따금씩은 자신의 처지나 고르지 못한 세상에 불평을 늘어놓기도 하고 또 걸어오는 시비는 구태여 마다하지 않고, 비록 변두리의 별 세 개짜리 호텔이긴 하지만 월말이면 꼬박꼬박 나오는 봉급에 손님들의 팁과 몸파는 아가씨들에게서 얻어먹는 구전까지 합치면 한 달 수입 삼십만 원은 되고, 그 가운데 매달 이십만 원은 어김없이 집으로 가져가 이제는 막일도 어려워진 중늙은이가 된 아버지와 어떤 시장 모퉁이에서 좌판을 벌이고 있는 어머니를 감격시키는, 강서호텔 육백 칠호실 벨보이 김시욱(金時旭) 군은 천구백팔십이년 십일월 이십육일 오후 여섯시 사십칠분쯤 이렇게 말했다.

"잡것들. 대낮부터 요란스럽기는 지금이 어떤 때라고……."

이문열 단편 소설 『두 겹의 노래』 해설
On Yi Mun-yol's short story, *Twofold Song*

"삶은 쓸쓸하다. 또는 쓸쓸하지 않다."로 시작되는 이 소설은, 사랑과 욕망과 이별을 통하여 우리의 삶과 이 세상이 두 겹으로 되어 있음을 말한다. 삶은 쓸쓸함과 쓸쓸하지 않음의 두 겹으로 되어 있고, 세상은 남자와 여자라는 두 겹으로 되어 있다. 남자와 여자가 만나 겹을 이루면 그것은 사랑이 된다. 그러나 사랑 속에서 수많은 두 겹이 있기에 언제나 한 겹이 되고자 하는 사랑을 좌절시킨다.

나무들이 잔인한 겨울의 예감으로 불안하게 일렁이는 쓸쓸한 가을날 오후, 남자와 여자는 공원의 벤치에 앉아 있다. 지난 삼 년간 사귀어 온 그들은 이제 헤어지려 한다. 그들의 대화는 공허하고 자꾸만 어긋난다. 남자가 눈을 이야기하면 여자는 햇빛을 이야기한다. 이어서 남자와 여자는 자신들의 만남에 대해 두 겹으로 노래한다. 처음 만날 무렵 남자의 외로움은 "고귀하고 성실한 영혼이 아니면 풍길 수 없는 재스민 향과도 같은 상심과 외로움"이기도 하고 또 "비뚤어진 욕정의 냄새"이기도 하다. 또 옛날 여자의 모습은 "눈이 부실 지경"으로 아름답기도 하고 또 아름다움으로 착각되는 "시들기 직전의 처연함"이기도 하다. 그들이 만났던 시간들은 "세월의 낭비"이기도 하고 또 "의미로 채워진 세월"이기도 하며, 그들이 도덕적이 된다는 것은 불륜의 관계를 끝내고 "우리를 비워 남으로 채우는 것"을 뜻하기도 하고 또 서로에게 충실하며 "자유로운 우리를 채우는 것"을 뜻하기도 한다. 이렇게 두 남녀는 헤어짐을 앞두고 서로 섞일 수 없는 두 겹의 노래를 부른다.

그러나 남녀의 사랑에는 우울한 사유만 있는 것이 아니고 달아오르는 육체도 있다. 이제 사유는 끝나고 "그 둘의 발밑에서 귀엽고 색정적인 사향노루 한 쌍이 불쑥 솟아" 오른다. 남자는 길거리의 아스팔트 껍질을 벗기고 그 자리에 "대지의 뼈"를 모아 담을 둘러 성합의 장소를 만든다. 거기서 그들은 "잃어버린 원초의 고향"을 회상한다. 그들은 현실을 잊고, 원초의 고향 속에서 온갖 동물이 된다. 그들이 성합을 하는 순간만은, 현실의 모든 속박으로부터 자유롭다. 육체가 대화를 나눌 때, 현실과 도덕과 질서와 생각 같은 것들은 잠시 사라지고 세상은 원시의 생명력으로 넘친다. 그들은 대지를 파헤치고 시간을 마음대로 넘나든다. 남자와 여자가 함께 욕망의 포로가 되었을 때 그들은 한 겹이지만, 그러나 욕망이 해소되면 그들은 다시 두 겹이 된다. 남녀의 사랑은 복잡한 사유와 단순한 육체의 두 겹으로 되어 있는 것이다.

성합이 끝나자 그들은 다시 차가운 현실로 돌아온다. 육체의 대화가 끝나고 다시 이별의 대화를 나눈다. 남자는 다시 석고상처럼 차가워지고 여자의 눈도 열린 창처럼 공허해진다. 남자에게 여자는 성녀이기도 했고 요부이기도 했다. 마찬가지로 여자에게 남자는 기사이기도 했고 치한이기도 했다. 그들의 사랑은 축복이면서 저주였고, 기쁨인 동시에 괴로움이었으며, 도취면서 환멸이었다. 두 사람은 모든 노래가 두 겹임을 확인하면서 마지막으로 메마른 키스를 하고 헤어진다. 서로 완전한 타인이 됨으로써 한때 그토록 열정적이었고, 절실했고, 아름다웠던 두 사람의 사랑의 노래는 끝난다.

그러나 두 겹의 노래는 여기서 끝나는 것이 아니다. 작가는 그들의 사랑을 둘러 싼 또 다른 두 겹을 보여준다. 그들이 잠시 머물며 사랑을 나누었던 호텔의 벨보이 청년의 노래는 두 남녀가 불렀던 노래와 전혀 다르다. 벨보이의 구차한 현실에서 볼 때 그들의 사랑은 난잡한 치정에 불과하다.

당사자에게는 아름답고 절실한 사랑도, 다른 사람의 눈에는 추한 욕정으로 비칠 수 있음을 작가는 지적한다.

아, 사랑에는 이렇게 많은 두 겹이 있고, 그 두 겹 사이는 낭떠러지처럼 아득하기 만한 것인가! 이 소설은 사랑에 대한 가장 우울한 진단서 가운데 하나일 것이다.

Beginning with "Life is loneliness. Or it is not loneliness," *Twofold Song* talks about love and desire to show us that our lives and the world we live in are composed of twofolds. Our lives are twofold in that they can be both lonely and not lonely. The world is twofold in that it consists of men and women. When a man meets a woman and together they create a fold, it is called love. The infinite twofoldness of love, however, frustrates lovers who want to become and remain onefold.

On a lonely autumn afternoon, as the trees toss about with the premonition of a vicious winter, a man and a woman are sitting on a bench. They are about to end their three-year relationship as their empty conversation constantly goes amiss. If the man talks about the snow, the woman talks about the sunlight. Then they begin to sing twofold about their first encounter. The man's loneliness as the woman first saw it is "the loneliness and sorrow like the scent of jasmine, which can only come from a noble and honest soul," but to the man, it is only "the smell of twisted desire." On the other hand, the woman's beauty that once "dazzled" the man is to here merely a "flower's sorrow just before it withers" mistaken for beauty.

Furthermore, the time they spent together is both "time wasted," yet "time filled with meaning."

Their becoming moral is to end their illicit affair and to "empty ourselves and fill the void with others." Or it is to be faithful to each other and to "fill the freed selves." In this way, the man and the woman sing the twofold song that cannot be mingled as they anticipate their separation.

The love between the man and the woman, however, not only involves gloomy thoughts but also the burning flesh of the bodies. Thus, their thoughts end and "two lovely and lustful musk deer springs out from beneath their feet." The man peels off pieces of asphalt from the road and gathers "the bones of the Earth" to build a wall and create a place for sexual union. There they reminisce about "the lost homeland of the primordial beginning." They forget their reality and become all kinds of animals in their original homeland. At least in the moment of their sexual union, the man and the woman are both freed from all fetters of their reality. When their flesh converse with each other, reality, morals, order, and thoughts disappear momentarily and the world overflows with a primordial life force. They dig the Earth and travel freely through time. They are one fold when they both become slaves to desire but once desire is spent they revert to being twofold. In short, the love between the man and the woman is twofold as it consists of both complex thoughts and simple flesh.

Upon the completion of their sexual union, the man and the woman return to reality. The conversation of the body ends and resumes the conversation of the farewell. Thus the man becomes as cold as a plaster statue and the eyes of the woman become as void as an open window. The woman was a saint and a temptress to the man as the man was a knight and a creep to the woman. Their love was at the same time a blessing and a curse, a joy and an affliction, or an intoxication and disillusionment.

In the end, they confirm that all songs are twofold and share a final dry kiss to bid farewell to each other. Their song of love, which was once so passionate, earnest, and beautiful, reaches the end as they become complete strangers to each other.

However, *Twofold Song* does not end here but goes on to show us another twofoldness encircling the main characters—the contradiction of their song with that of the bellboy of the hotel where they made love. From the perspective of the bellboy's ordinary reality, their love is no more than a foolish lust, or passion. Love which seems so beautiful and earnest to one person can seem like a superficial and fleeting emotion to others.

Could it be true, then, that love has such an infinite twofoldness and that each of them are separated from one another by a vast expanse? If so, *Twofold Song* may be one of the darkest diagnoses of love.

이남호 · 문학평론가, 고려대학교 교수
Lee Nam-ho · Literary Critic and Professor at Korea University

현실과 환상을 넘나드는 두 겹의 그림
Twofold Illustrations of Reality and Fantasy

소설이 사랑을 둘러싼 두 겹의 노래를 논할 때 그림은 이 소설을 위해 어떠한 화음으로 두 겹의 노래를 연주할 수 있을 것인가. 일러스트레이터 곽선영은 현실 속에 벌어지는 남녀의 상황을 연극적인 설정을 통하여 현실 밖의 시공간 속으로 데려가는 시도를 한다.

황량한 초현실의 공간 속에 '남자 역'의 남자와 '여자 역'의 여자가 무대 위에 등장을 하고 이야기가 진행됨에 따라 어디서부턴가 자라나는 원시 정글 속 '본능'이 무대를 장식한다. 루소(Henri Rousseau)가 그렸던 이국적인 열대림 속, 혹은 대지 위에 잠든 집시의 꿈 속을 옮겨다 놓은 듯, 원시 자연 속에 한 겹이 된 암컷과 숫컷은 두 겹으로 엇갈리는 모든 '관념'의 노래를 잠시 접고 신성하리만큼 격렬한 성합의 노래를 부른다. 그 순간 곽선영의 그림 속에서 각기 열 개의 팔다리를 부여받은 암컷과 수컷의 싱싱한 몸짓은 명쾌함 그 자체이다.

절정의 순간이 지나자 어디에서부터인가 자라난 고독이

무대 위의 울창했던 원시림을 황량하게 하고 남과 여는 다시 '남자 역'의 또한 '여자 역'의 가면 뒤로 숨어 버린다. 무대의 이쪽과 저쪽에 나뉘어 서서 저마다의 노래를 부르던 목소리가 점점 사라지고 무대 위에는 '남'과 '여'의 황량했던 자취만이 남는다.

현실이 남긴 환상에 대한 목마름도, 환상이 되돌려준 현실에 대한 배반감도 잠깐, 남과 여는 무엇에도 갈등하지 않으며 자기만의 공간 속에 자기만의 방식대로 살아가는 것만이 유일한 방법임을 확인하며 저마다의 '별'로 귀환하기위해 날아가 버린다. 그것은 영원히 두 겹으로 존재할 수 밖에 없는 남과 여의 노래에 대한 여운으로 연극적인 설정의 피날레를 장식한다.

곽선영의 그림은, 글과의 묘한 화음 또는 불협화음을 만들어 내며 글을 배척하지도 글에 종속되지도 않는 완벽한 두 겹의 악보를 연주하고 있다.

In order to harmonize visual images with the twofold song of love, Kwak Sun-young creates vivid illustrations of a theatrical nature, while luring readers into time and space which exist outside of their reality.

A man and a woman for the role of 'man' and 'woman' appear on the stage that seems both desolate and surreal. As their story progresses, a primordial jungle quickly penetrates the stage and its 'instinct' decorates the center. Here, the man and the woman set aside all misconceived twofold songs of 'ideology' and they become onefold to sing a sacred song of violent sexual consummation. The primordial nature, like that of Henri Rousseau's paintings of the gypsy's dreams and the exotic tropical forests, surrounds them. Kwak Sun-young bestows ten arms and legs upon the man and the woman, as each body movement becomes filled with life and energy.

Loneliness grows soon after the man and the woman have reached climax. Desolation advances to the stage recapturing the 'reality' of the dense jungle. Both the man and the woman hide behind the masks of the roles they had been playing initially, that of the 'man' and 'woman' respectively. Singing voices from the opposite ends of the stage dissipate and the empty shells of the 'man' and the 'woman' linger on.

Even the craving for fantasy and sense of betrayal both induced by the return of reality are short-lived. The man and the woman assure themselves that they can live solely within the confinement of their own space, by their own rules, and in the absence of any possible conflict. They proceed to fly away and return to their respective 'stars,' adorning the final stage scene with the resonance of their song that would forever remain twofold.

The illustrations of Kwak Sun-young create both consonance and dissonance as twofold musical notes neither alienate nor succumb to the story of *Twofold Song*.

이나미 · 북프로듀서, 크리에이티브 디렉터/스튜디오 바프
Rhee Nami · Book Producer and Creative Director at Studio BAF